Once upon a time, there lived a frog in a beautiful pound. But it is not just another frog that you see in another pound.

It is larger than a usual frog. It is more colorful than the others. Its eyes glow red color.

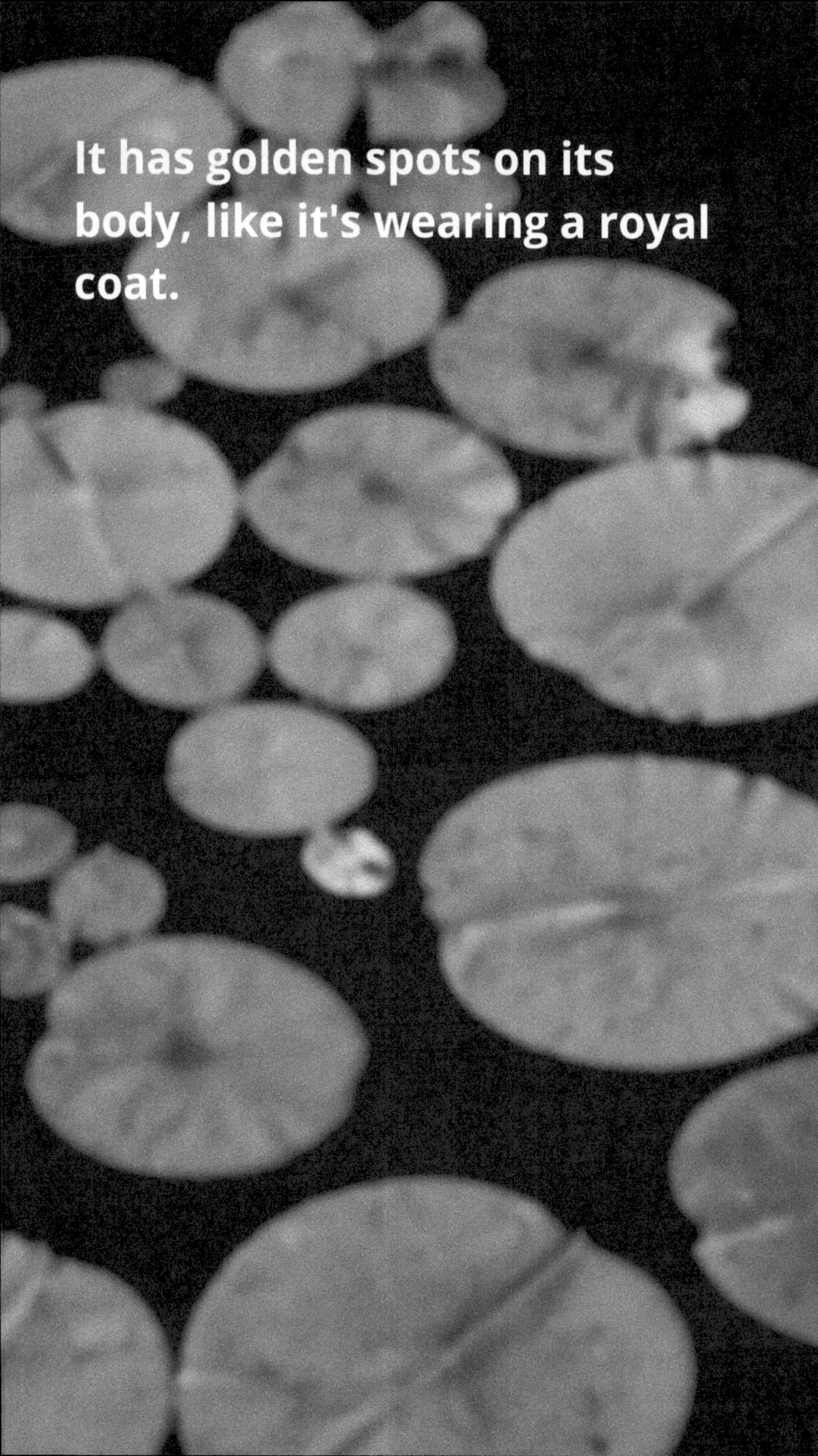
It has golden spots on its body, like it's wearing a royal coat.

It's legs and hands had sharp finger nails that you can't see. The nails appear when they are needed and disappear.

And it can jump a longer distance than the others. And the most important thing is that this frog doesn't eat any insects in the daytime or at night.

This is how you see the frog in the daytime.
When the evening comes,

this frog disappears from the pond. You'll not be able to find it in the pond at night.

Now you may wonder!
So where does it go?
What does it do at night?
What does it eat to live?

Here's what happens when the sun goes down and the evening comes the frog goes to a nearby caravan and gets bigger to the size of a human and turns into a human.

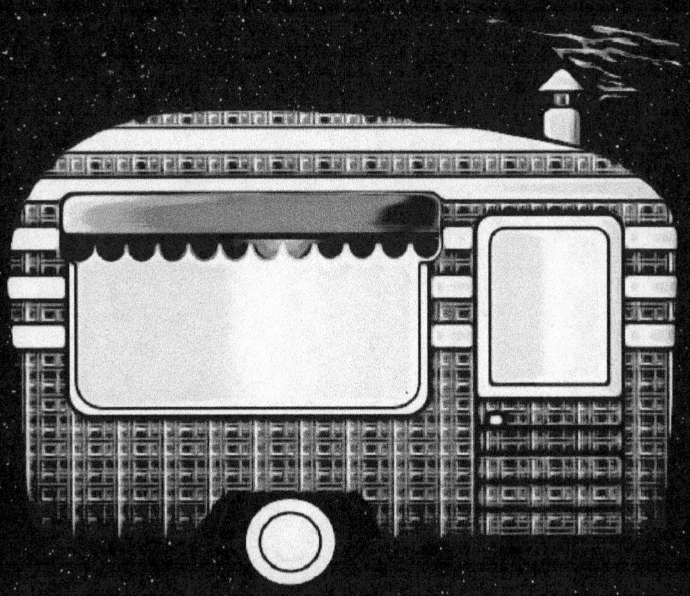

But it can't hide that it's a frog. It's face still looks like a frog.
Then this frog starts singing songs.

Its voice is like a Chinese man. and starts cooking food that no one knows what it's cooking.

And when someone gets near this caravan the frog senses it and the door opens automatically.

And with its special power the frog attracts the humans into the caravan and offers the food which it prepared to the human.

The food taste delicious. You have never experienced anything so tasty and delicious before.

However this frog only invites one human at once to this caravan.
So what happens to this human?

After the human eat the delicious food the frog puts the human in a deep sleep and let the human see sweet dreams that you have never seen before.

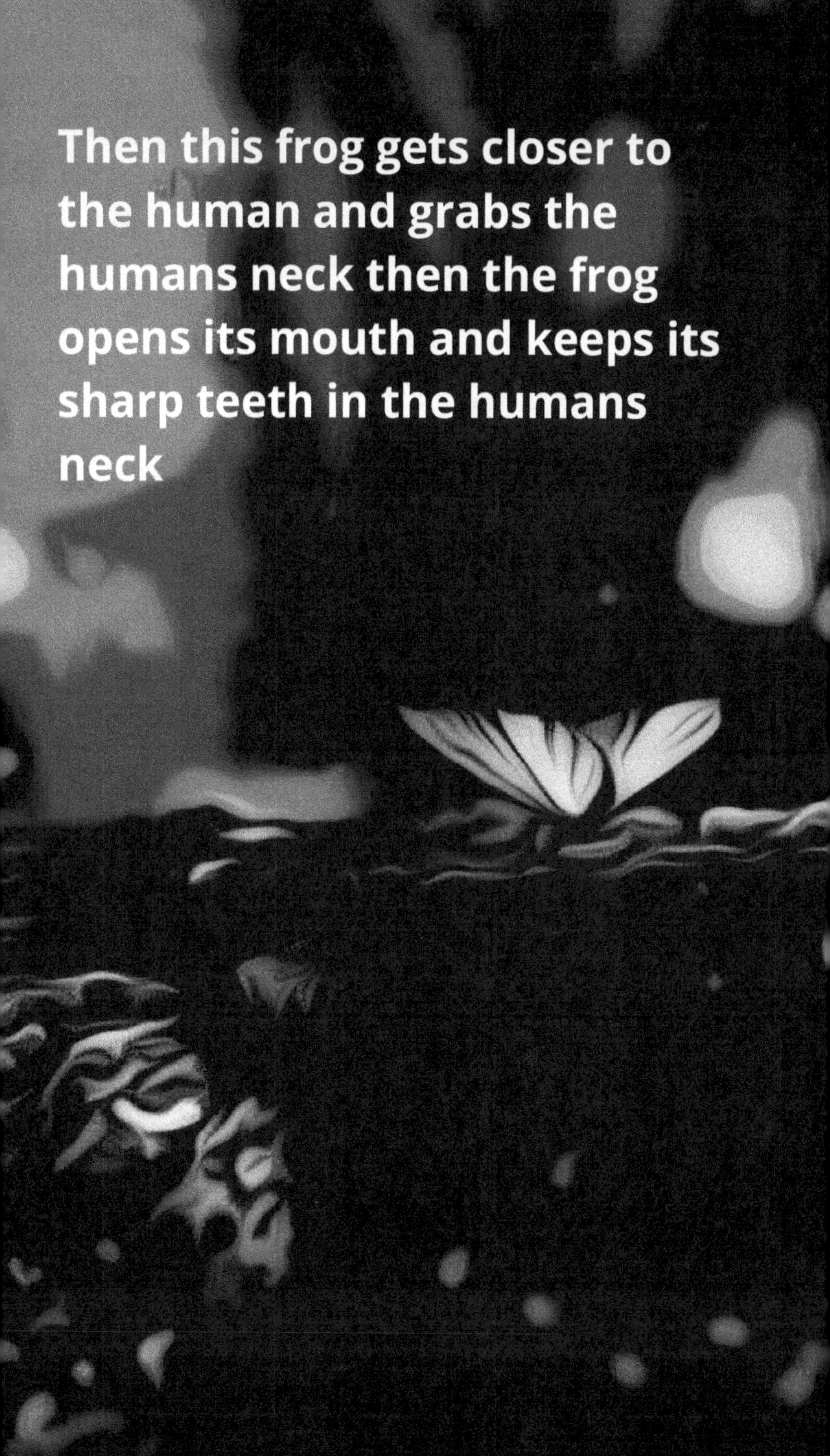
Then this frog gets closer to the human and grabs the humans neck then the frog opens its mouth and keeps its sharp teeth in the humans neck

then It injects its venom and starts drinking the human blood.But it only drinks a small amount of blood.

Then in the dawn time before the sun rises the vampire frog releases the human.

And the human sleep walks home to sleep in his own bed.

And When the sun rises the vampire frog will turn back into a unique beautiful frog and go back to the pond.

The human will wake up in the late morning feeling dizzy but the human will not remember what actually happened at night.

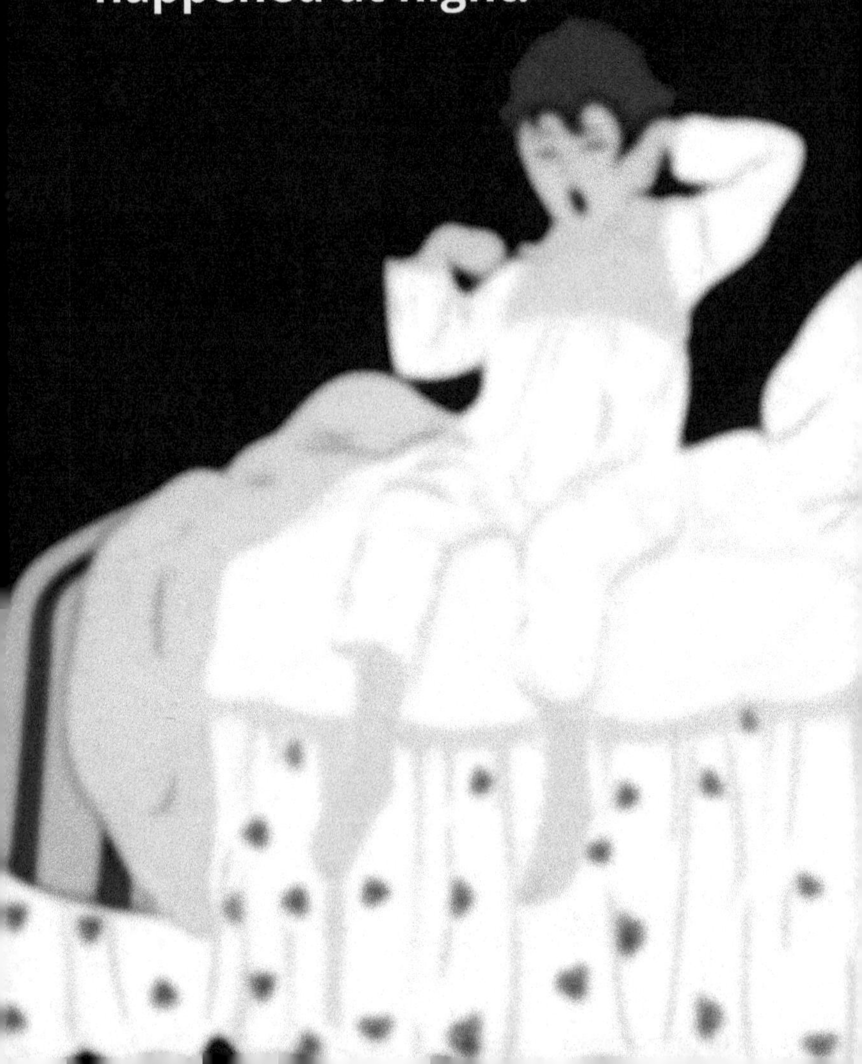

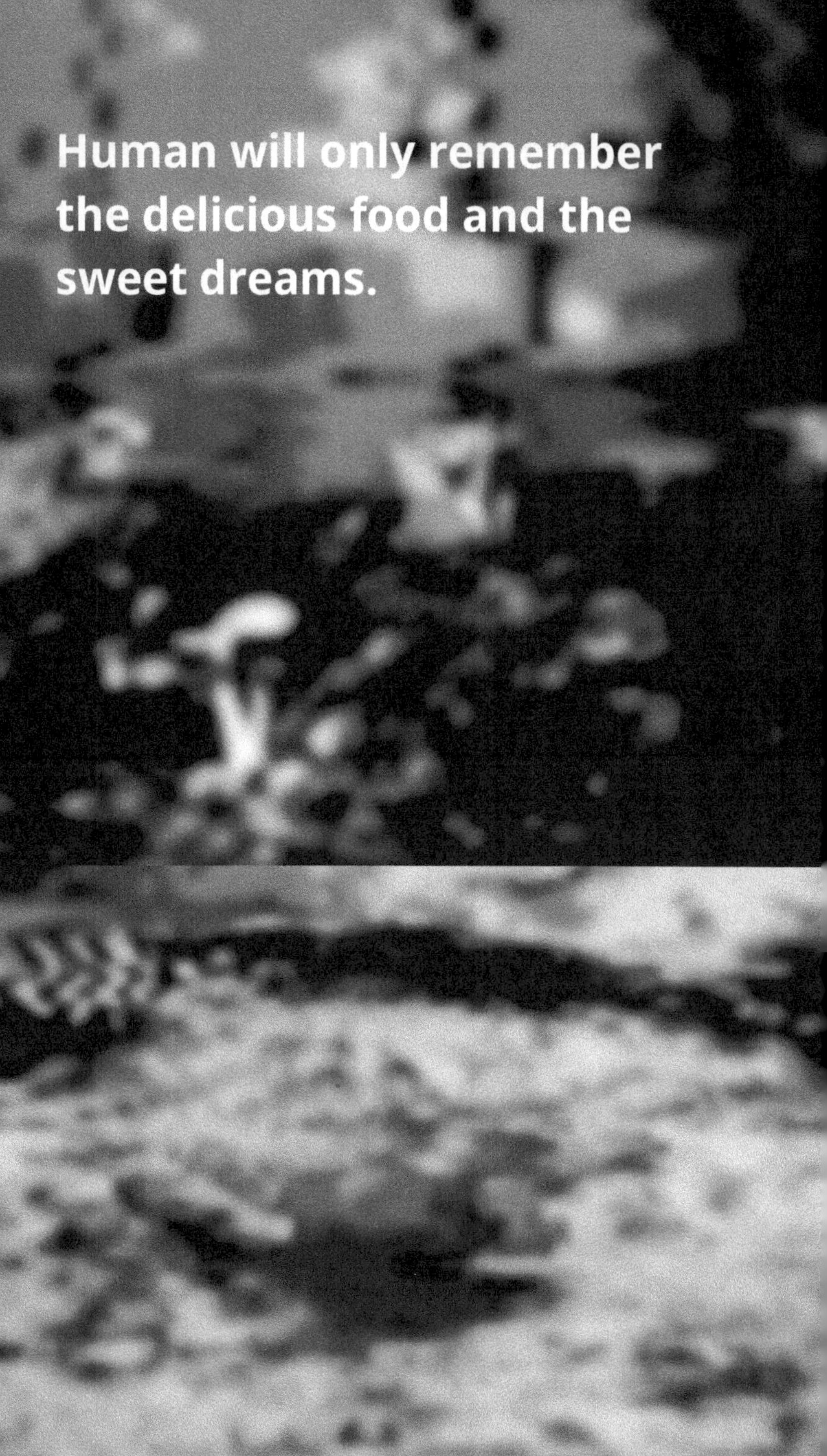
Human will only remember
the delicious food and the
sweet dreams.

And the frog lives an immortal life of eternity

The End

www.ingramcontent.com/pod-product-compliance
Lightning Source LLC
La Vergne TN
LVHW020546160826
845677LV00015B/4229

* 9 7 9 8 8 4 4 2 0 3 1 9 0 *